The Little Beaver

Written by Christopher Jordan ❧ Illustrated by Stephanie Boey

Deep within a lush forest of towering trees and clear mountain streams, lived a community of animals. During the warm summer months, Bear, Moose, Eagle, Owl and Rabbit frolicked in the lush meadows and played amid the swaying trees, all while Little Beaver watched from a lonely distance, atop his home made of logs. He longed for their friendship, but he was too shy to approach them. He didn't live where they lived, nor did he look the same. He felt very different from the others.

As Autumn came, Little Beaver watched as the others gathered food to store for the approaching winter. As the colourful leaves began to fall from the trees, he thought about helping and saying hello, but he couldn't find the courage.

"Maybe," he thought, "Maybe, I'll say hello tomorrow."

But when tomorrow came, the snow began to fall and the forest was covered in a world of white. Coming out of his lodge, Little Beaver hardly recognized the place where he lived.

The meadow was a white field of deep, deep snow, the trees of the wood heavily laden. Nothing moved and the long, cold months of winter settled in.
Little Beaver stayed in his home.

As the months became warmer and the short dark days brightened, the snow began to melt and the forest became damp. The rain fell and the rivers and streams began to swell. From inside his lodge, Little Beaver heard an unfamiliar sound; a dripping noise, as the ice covering his roof began to melt.

Then, he heard something else. A cry!

Little Beaver scampered up to the top of his wood lodge where he saw Eagle soaring high above, calling down to the animals.

"The snow is melting far upstream!" he cried. "The river is overflowing and there is going to be a flood!"

Hearing Eagle's desperate warning, the animals began to panic.

"**What** shall we do?" said Moose.

"Our homes will be **washed away!**" whimpered Rabbit.

Little Beaver heard their cries, and looking upstream he could see the water already rising. He knew there was something he could do. After all, he **was** a Beaver.

Little Beaver gathered his courage and hurried across the meadow to the animals. He longed for their friendship and wanted to offer his help. Without fear, he said, "A dam. We must build a dam!"

Moose thought it was a great idea, but said, "We don't know how."

"No," said Little Beaver, "But I do. If we all work together, we can build a dam strong enough to hold back the flood and save your homes."

Little Beaver told the animals what to do. Eagle and Owl flew high, searching for the best trees and branches. Bear and Moose dragged them back to the riverbank while Little Beaver worked with the other animals, and the dam began to take shape. They worked together through the day and night until confident they could do no more.

"Quick!" cried Eagle, from high in the sky, "the water is coming!"

Before they could see anything, there was a great rushing noise from upstream and then the water came hurtling down the valley. The dam looked high and strong, but would it hold the floodwater back? Would it save their homes?

The water raced closer and closer to the dam, then swelled as it met the great wooden wall. The animals huddled in fear, though Little Beaver stood secure. He knew they had built a good dam.

The dam **creaked** and **moaned** against the weight of the water, but held strong. Their homes had been saved and Little Beaver was a hero. One by one all the animals thanked and congratulated him.

"Thank you, Little Beaver," they cried. "Without you our homes would have been washed away."

Little Beaver began to realize how foolish his shyness had been. And the others realized that while each animal was different, they were all equally the same. From that day on they celebrated Beaver's clever thinking and how his courage not only saved the day, but created new and everlasting friendships.